Eloise Greenfield

Honey, I Love

illustrations by
Jan Spivey Gilchrist

HarperCollins*Publishers*

Amistad

Amistad is an imprint of HarperCollins Publishers, Inc.

Honey, I Love
Text copyright © 1978 by Eloise Greenfield
Illustrations copyright © 2003 by Jan Spivey Gilchrist
Manufactured in China. All rights reserved.
www.harperchildrens.com

Library of Congress Cataloging-in-Publication Data
Greenfield, Eloise.
Honey, I love / by Eloise Greenfield ; illustrations by Jan Spivey Gilchrist.— 1st ed.
p.   cm.
Summary: A young girl expresses what she loves about life.
ISBN 0-06-009123-1 — ISBN 0-06-009124-X (lib. bdg.)
1. African American girls—Juvenile poetry.   2. Children's poetry, American.
[1. African Americans—Poetry.   2. American poetry.]
I. Gilchrist, Jan Spivey, ill.   II. Title.
PS3557.R39416 H656   2003   811'.54—dc21   2002001464

1 2 3 4 5 6 7 8 9 10   ❖   First Edition

Text originally published by
Thomas Y. Crowell in *Honey, I Love and Other Love Poems*

To my uncle and aunt,
Frank Sr. and Athalene Emory
—E.G.

For my precious granddaughter,
Raena Bethany,
and her beautiful mother,
my daughter, Ronké
—J.S.G.

I love
I love a lot of things,
a whole lot of things
Like . . .

My cousin comes to visit
and you know he's from the South
'cause every word he says
just kind of slides out of his mouth

I like the way
he whistles
and I like the way
he walks

But honey, let me tell you that
I LOVE the way he talks
I love the way my cousin talks
  and

The day is hot and icky
and the sun sticks to my skin
Mr. Davis turns the hose on,
everybody jumps right in
The water stings my stomach
and I feel so nice and cool

Honey, let me tell you
that I LOVE a flying pool
I love to feel a flying pool
and

Renee comes out to play
and brings her doll without a dress

I make a dress with paper
and that doll sure looks a mess

We laugh so loud and long and hard
the doll falls to the ground
Honey, let me tell you that
I LOVE the laughing sound
I love to make the laughing sound
  and

My uncle's car is crowded
and there's lots of food to eat
We're going down the country
where the church folks like to meet

I'm looking out the window
at the cows and trees outside

Honey, let me tell you that
I LOVE to take a ride
I love to take a family ride
and

My mama's on the sofa
sewing buttons on my coat
I go and sit beside her,
I'm through playing with my boat

I hold her arm and kiss it
'cause it feels so soft and warm
Honey, let me tell you that
I LOVE my mama's arm
I love to kiss my mama's arm
and

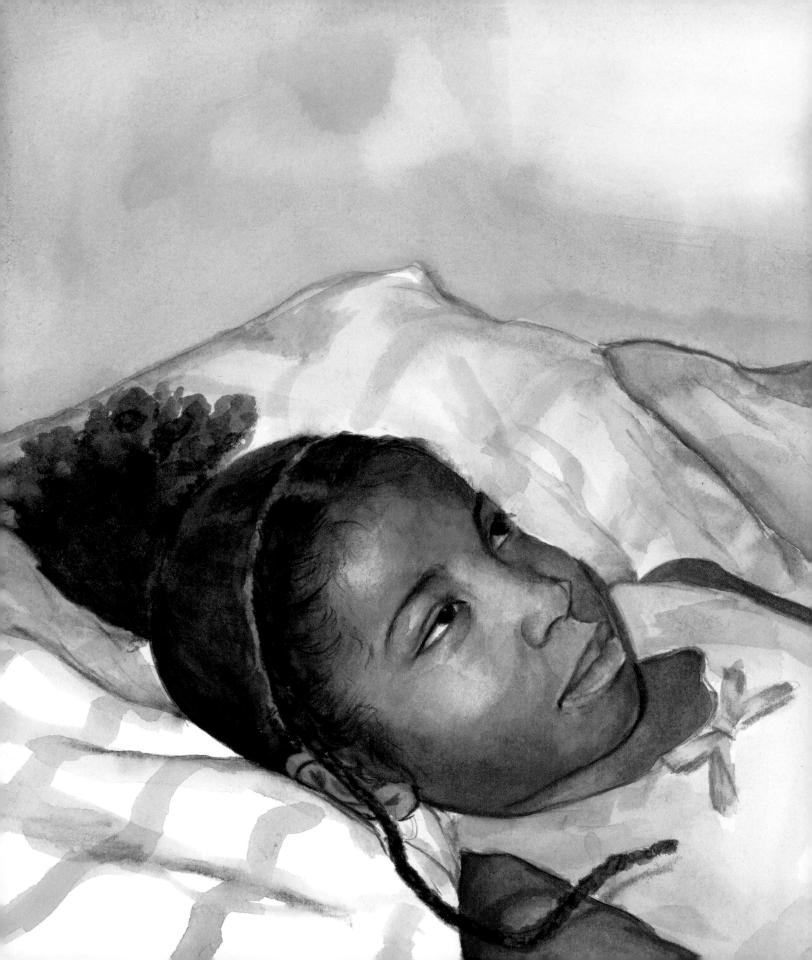

It's not so late at night,
but still I'm lying in my bed
I guess I need my rest,
at least that's what my mama said

She told me not to cry
'cause she don't want to hear a peep
Honey, let me tell you
I DON'T love to go to sleep
I do not love to go to sleep

But I love
I love a lot of things,
a whole lot of things

And honey,
I love ME, too.